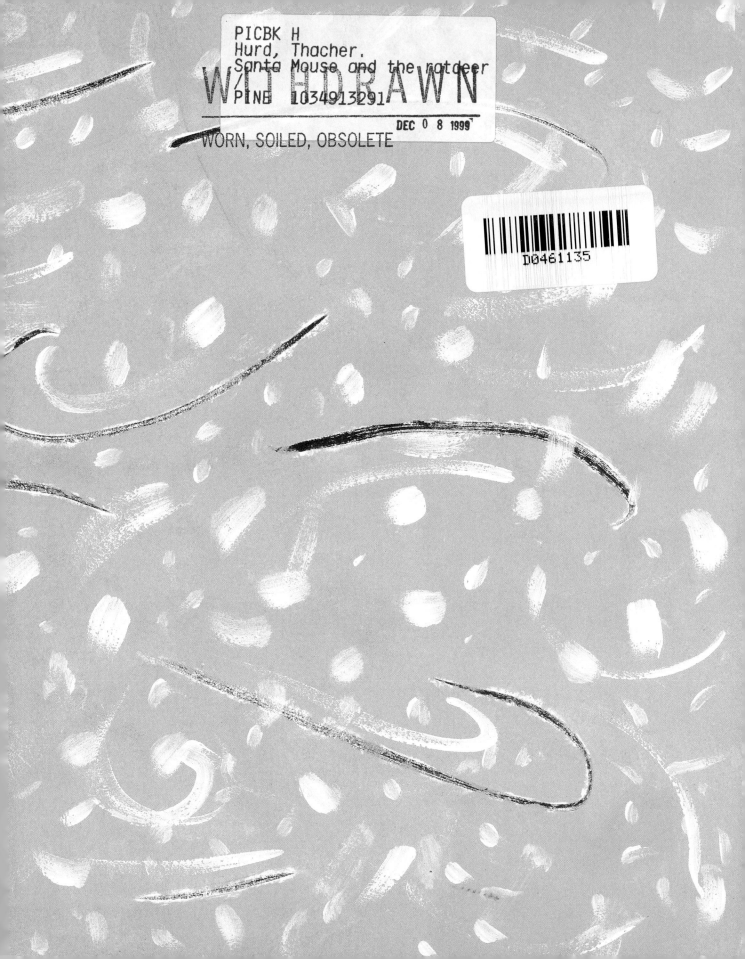

# Santa Mouse and the Ratdeer

## by

## Thacher Hurd

HarperCollins Publishers

It was Christmas Eve.

Father and Mother Mouse and Rosie

were decorating their Christmas tree.

Father Mouse was trying to make the lights work,

and Mother was untangling the tinsel.

Rosie was putting a star on top of the tree.

"Be careful," said Mother Mouse,

just as Rosie . . .

fell off the ladder—
*SWOOSH!*
and almost knocked over
the Christmas tree.

*THUMP!* Rosie fell into the box of tinsel.

"Yikes!" cried Mother.

"Rosie, let's finish making those cookies," said Father.

"Santa Mouse is coming soon."

But at the Mouse North Pole
Santa Mouse was having a hard time.
He was late.
"Where's my map!

Where's my underwear? Where are my socks?

I thought my hat was right here!"

Santa couldn't even get his boots on.

Finally Santa was ready.

He started loading presents.

"Oh, no! I forgot to fix the sleigh!

No time for that now."

Santa was in a bad mood.

Santa's ratdeer were grumbling too:

"On Blunder! On Basher!

On Lousy and Loopy and Bugsy and Twizzlebum!"

Santa Mouse and the ratdeer took off.

It was a dark and snowy night.

The wind blew snow and ice into Santa's face.

It felt like icicles stabbing him.

Before he knew what had happened . . .

. . . the wind had torn Santa's map out of his paws.
As he tried to grab the map,
his lunch box and his thermos of hot chocolate
also disappeared down into the storm.
Then his sleigh started to malfunction.
It pitched and yawed and fell

   down

       down

           down . . .

CRASH! into a snowbank in the middle of the North Woods.

Presents were scattered everywhere.

"What a disaster!" said Santa.

The ratdeer were at the end of their rope too.

The ratdeer climbed out of the snow

and marched off into the woods.

*"Brrrrrr."* Santa shivered and looked around.

He was cold and hungry,

and lost in the woods with a broken sleigh.

Meanwhile, Rosie wanted to make sure
that Santa would find her house.
"Rosie!" Mother called. "Time for bed!"

Rosie went inside and put on her nightie.

Mother tucked her into bed.

The moon rose, and the sky cleared.

Soon everyone was asleep.

But in the middle of the night Rosie woke up.

She heard a scratching at the door. What was that?

It was the ratdeer. They were shivering. They were bedraggled.

"Who are you?" asked Rosie.

"Blunder and Basher and Lousy and Loopy
and Bugsy and Twizzlebum."

"We're lost," said Loopy.

"We were looking for the beach," said Blunder.

"There's no beach around here," said Rosie.

"How about some cookies?"

The ratdeer nodded.

"Some hot chocolate?" said Rosie.

The ratdeer nodded.

"A toasty fire?"

The ratdeer smiled.

"Gee, Bugsy, Santa might like a cookie too."

"Yeah, but he's still in the woods," said Twizzlebum.

Bugsy and Twizzlebum went back to find Santa.

Where was he?

Then they heard something:

It was Santa, singing in the woods.

"Want some hot chocolate, Santa?" asked Bugsy.

"Sounds good."

Bugsy and Twizzlebum brought Santa back to Rosie's house.

The cookies were warm.

The chocolate was hot.

Santa Mouse told a joke. Rosie laughed.

The ratdeer laughed.

Santa and Rosie and the ratdeer went back to the sleigh.

Santa took out his toolbox and fixed the malfunction.

Then he put all the presents, except one, back in the sleigh.

"Here—this present is for you," said Santa to Rosie.

"Wow!" said Rosie. "And I found *this* in the snow."

"Great! I need that!" said Santa. "It's my map."

Rosie waved good-bye as Santa took off.
"So long, Blunder and Basher and
Lousy and Loopy and Bugsy and Twizzlebum!"

On Christmas morning

Father, Mother, and Rosie were opening presents.

Father asked Rosie,

"Where did that little sleigh come from?"

Then Mother asked Rosie,

"And who drank all the hot chocolate?"

Rosie just smiled.

# Mouse Prayer at Christmas

May all mice be cozy,

may all mice be warm,

may all mice have friendship

and a place to call home.

Let foxes be gone

and cats be asleep,

let mousetraps be broken

and honey be sweet.

Sing for joy,

sing for good cheer,

sing for Santa

and his ridiculous ratdeer.

*Many thanks to Olivia, Robert, Sharon, and the Tuesday Group. Thanks also to Sonny for Santa Mouse's joke.*

Knock knock. Who's there? Noel. Noel who? No elbows on the table!